Dear Parents and Teachers,

In an easy-reader format, **My Readers** introduce classic stories to children who are learning to read. Favorite characters and time-tested tales are the basis for **My Readers**, which are available in three levels:

1 **Level One** is for the emergent reader and features repetitive language and word clues in the illustrations.

2 **Level Two** is for more advanced readers who still need support saying and understanding some words. Stories are longer with word clues in the illustrations.

3 **Level Three** is for independent, fluent readers who enjoy working out occasional unfamiliar words. The stories are longer and divided into chapters.

Encourage children to select books based on interests, not reading levels. Read aloud with children, showing them how to use the illustrations for clues. With adult guidance and rereading, children will eventually read the desired book on their own.

Here are some ways you might want to use this book with children:

- Talk about the title and the cover illustrations. Encourage the child to use these to predict what the story is about.
- Discuss the interior illustrations and try to piece together a story based on the pictures. Does the child want to change or adjust his first prediction?
- After children reread a story, suggest they retell or act out a favorite part.

My Readers will not only help children become readers, they will serve as an introduction to some of the finest classic children's books available today.

—LAURA ROBB
Educator and Reading Consultant

For activities and reading tips, visit myreadersonline.com

For Esmé, who carries
little wandering good feelings
in her tiny pocket

SQUARE
FISH
An Imprint of Macmillan Children's Publishing Group

Printed in August 2011 in China by Toppan Leefung Printing Ltd., Dongguan City, Guangdong Province.
For information, address Square Fish, 175 Fifth Avenue, New York, NY 10010.

Library of Congress Cataloging-in-Publication Data
Hoban, Russell.
The little brute family / story by Russell Hoban : pictures by Lillian Hoban.
p. cm.
Summary: Members of the Brute family, who live on a diet of stick and stone stew,
suddenly find their lives changed for the better.

ISBN 978-0-312-62138-4 (hardcover)
1 3 5 7 9 10 8 6 4 2

ISBN 978-0-312-56373-8 (paperback)
1 3 5 7 9 10 8 6 4 2

I. Hoban, Lillian, ill. II. Title.
PZ7. H637 Li 2002   [E]—dc21   2001054748

Originally published in the United States by Macmillan
First MY READERS Edition: 2011

Square Fish logo designed by Filomena Tuosto

Book design by Patrick Collins/Véronique Lefèvre Sweet

myreadersonline.com
mackids.com

This is a Level 2 book

AR: 4.4

The Little Brute Family

Story by **Russell Hoban**
Pictures by **Lillian Hoban**

**SQUARE
FISH**

Macmillan Children's Publishing Group
New York

In the middle of a dark
and shadowy woods
lived a little family of Brutes.

There were Papa Brute, Mama Brute,

Brother and Sister Brute,

and Baby Brute.

In the morning
Mama cooked
a sand and gravel porridge,
and the family snarled and grimaced
as they spooned it up.

No one said, "Please."

No one said, "Thank you,"

and no one said,

"How delicious,"

because it was not delicious.

Baby Brute howled between spoonfuls.

Brother and Sister kicked

each other under the table,

and Mama and Papa

made faces

while they ate.

After breakfast Papa Brute

took up his sack

and went to gather sticks and stones.

Mama stayed home

to thump the furniture

and bang the pots

and scold the baby.

And Brother and Sister
pushed and shoved
and punched and pinched
their way to school.

In the evenings Mama served
a stew of sticks and stones,
and the family ate it
with growls and grumbling.

Then they groaned and went to sleep.

That was how they lived.

They never laughed

and said, "Delightful!"

They never smiled

and said, "How lovely!"

17

In the spring

the little Brutes made heavy kites

that bumped along the ground

and would not fly.

In the summer

they flung themselves into the pond

and sank like stones

but never learned to swim.

In the fall

they jumped into great piles of leaves

and stamped on one another, yelling.

In the winter

they leaped upon

their crooked clumsy sleds

that took them crashing into snowbanks

where they stuck headfirst

and screamed.

That was how they lived

in the dark and shadowy woods.

Then one day Baby Brute found

a little wandering lost good feeling

in a field of daisies,

and he caught it in his paw

and put it in his tiny pocket.

And he felt so good

that he laughed and said,

"How lovely."

Baby Brute felt good all afternoon,
and at supper
when his bowl was filled with stew
he said, "Thank you."

Then the little good feeling

flew out of his tiny pocket

and hovered over the table,

humming and smiling.

"How lovely!" said Mama,

without even snarling.

"Delightful!" said Papa,

forgetting to growl.

"Oh, please," said all

the little Brutes together,

"let it stay with us!"

And Papa smiled and said, "All right."

When Papa Brute went out

for sticks and stones the next day,

he found wild berries,

salad greens, and honey,

and he brought them home instead.

At supper everyone said,

"How delicious!"

because it *was* delicious,

and everyone said,

"Please" and "Thank you."

And they never ate

stick and stone stew again.

Then the little good feeling

stopped wandering

and stayed with the little Brute family.

When springtime came

the little Brutes made bright new kites

that flew high in the sky,

and in the summer

they swam beautifully.

In the fall

they gathered nuts and acorns

that they roasted by a cozy fire

when winter came.

And in the evening

they sang songs together.

The little good feeling stayed and stayed

and never went away,

and when springtime came again

the little Brute family

changed their name to Nice.